To Klaus & Nutmeg - the two reindeer who
changed our lives forever.

Donngggg.
Donnngggg.

The clock chimed twice. Just as it did, a knock at the door told the Snowmans their visitor had arrived. "Greetings, friend! Welcome to the place where **SNOWY SECRETS** are shared. Come in, and make yourself comfortable."

"We love having visitors, and you are just in time for a special treat. Every visitor gets to ask one special question about the North Pole that we promise to answer. Think carefully... what will your question be today?"

"Do reindeer REALLY fly?"

"Of course they do! But, they do
lots of other things too!" exclaimed
Mama Snowman.

TEAM SANTA

Mama Snowman began. "Each and every reindeer is special just like each and every one of you. We give reindeer their jobs based on their talents. We watch them from the time they are born to see what they do best. Reindeer that fly are what we call **TEAM SANTA REINDEER**. They are very competitive and play all kinds of sports. They are really good at sledding, skating, running, jumping, and, of course, flying."

Papa Snowman continued. "Santa selects special farmers throughout the world to help raise and train the **TEAM SANTA REINDEER**. When one of Santa's regular reindeer needs a break during their magical ride on Christmas Eve, Santa drops them off to rest while a **TEAM SANTA REINDEER** takes their place. By placing **TEAM SANTA REINDEER** all over the world, Santa can drop off and pick up reindeer anywhere he needs to, making the flight go VERY fast since all of his reindeer are rested, watered, and fed."

Papa Snowman kept going. "We all know the next type of reindeer because you may have a brother, sister, or friend like this. **JOKESTER REINDEER** make life fun and do all sorts of silly things that make us laugh. An example would be when a **JOKESTER REINDEER** sneaks up behind you and pokes you in the bottom with their antlers. Then everyone starts laughing so hard that it hurts."

"What is 5 x 1.9 billion?" asked Mama Snowman. "It's ok if you don't know the answer," said Mama. "Our **EINSTEIN REINDEER** are great at math! They calculate how many presents we need for all of the children in the world. They also help Santa with things like figuring out how much time he has at each house and where each child is located. A very famous reindeer with a red nose is this type of reindeer and helps Santa all year long. "

KERBOOM, CLANK, SWISH! A loud racket came from the kitchen that echoed all over the house. Papa Snowman marched into the room clanking together metal lids. He was followed by a reindeer pounding on a large drum with his hoof. Mama Snowman started laughing and said, "At the North Pole we have a special group that is called the North Pole Jazz BAM. That's right BAM, not BAND, because of the way they like to pound on all sorts of things to make music."

"**RHYTHM REINDEER** give us loud and joyous music all year long. It's never dull around here!"

Everyone jumped at the sound of yelling outside. "KNOCK IT OFF! Someone is going to lose an eye out there with all that antler clashing and head-butting. STOP IT RIGHT NOW I SAY!" "That is what we call a **BOSS REINDEER**," stated Papa Snowman. "**BOSS REINDEER** are take charge, no nonsense, my way or the highway, get things done types who keep everyone in line. Santa and reindeer farmers everywhere need **BOSS REINDEER** to make sure there isn't too much goofing around.

"HARK!" A reindeer leaped into the room throwing a scarf around his neck and waving a hoof in the air for dramatic flair. "Meet our **THEATRICAL REINDEER!**" said Papa Snowman. "What would life be like without the melodramatic telling of stories, puppetry, or acting out tales of Santa and his reindeer? Whether it is on the stage or big screen, **THEATRICAL REINDEER** give us great joy and entertainment," said Mama Snowman.

"Do you see those beautiful ornaments?" asked Papa Snowman. "Those are the work of our **ARTIST REINDEER** here at the North Pole. Santa believes that we should surround ourselves with beautiful things. Colorful costumes for the elves and reindeer show our holiday spirit. From cookies and cakes, to the sleigh, clothes, paintings, decorations and ornaments, the **ARTIST REINDEER** help make Christmas beautiful."

"Come with me to the window," said Mama Snowman as she moved across the room. As Mama Snowman opened the window and leaned out, two reindeer came running to greet her.

The first reindeer lifted his face up to hers. He softly kissed her cheek with his black lips and soft, white nose covered in tiny ice crystals.

She reached out and
gave him a big hug.

The other reindeer lovingly looked at Mama Snowman as she blew them a frosty kiss and called out, "I love you."

As she pulled inside and closed the window, Mama Snowman said, "You just met two of the most important types of reindeer in the entire world. These are **MAGICAL REINDEER**. Santa delivers these reindeer all over the world because they are so sweet and loving.

"**MAGICAL REINDEER** come in two forms. One is outgoing and shows their love by kissing your cheek and giving you hugs. The other loves you quietly and gently from afar. They listen to you when you are happy or sad so you never feel alone. Even though there are so many different types of reindeer, we love them all just the same," explained Mama Snowman.

"Remember the next time you see a reindeer, that they don't have to be a flying reindeer to be special and loved."

TEAM SNOWMA

"You just have to enjoy and love them for who they are," said Papa Snowman.

Donnngggg.
Donnnggggg.
Donnnggggg.

The clock's sweet melody reminded the visitor that it was time to go. Mama and Papa Snowman blew snowy kisses, saying, "Until we meet again."

As they watched out their door, Mama and Papa Snowman heard "CRUNCH, CRUNCH, CLICK, CLICK" as the **MAGICAL REINDEER** joined the visitor for the long journey home.

If you could visit Mama and Papa Snowman, what Snowy Secret would you like to know? Write your questions here or send them to:
mama@snowysecrets.com

Fun Tidbits:

The address where Mama and Papa Snowman live represents the year that author's Tracy and Scott Snowman adopted their first reindeer from the North Pole – 20**15**.

The head gear worn by Mama and Papa Snowman is the same as the favorite head gear worn in the winter by the authors.

The little gold tags seen on the halters of some of the reindeer throughout the book are hints about identity. For example, the reindeer with a "D" on his halter is Dasher. "B" is for Blitzen, "V" is for Vixen and "R" is for Rudolph. You will also notice that one of the pages has a reindeer with an "M", which stands for Mistletoe. Mistletoe is one of the author's reindeer who inspired two of the characters in the book: Boss Reindeer and Artist Reindeer.

Jokester Reindeer was inspired by one of the author's favorite reindeer who frequently nudges them in the bottom when working outside in the pasture. This little reindeer has a very playful personality. The real life reindeer's name is Kringle (after Kris Kringle).

There are several pages that feature Snowman cookies. These are references to the author's last name.

Tracy Snowman and grandson, Luke Scott, are featured in the barn scene with the Magical Reindeer. They are in the back of the scene. The illustration was done from an actual photograph of Luke getting kisses from their reindeer, Snowball. You will also notice that Luke Scott is written on the clock on the wall of the last page featuring Mama and Papa Snowman. Luke loves helping author Scott Snowman wind his antique clock so the actual clock from the Snowman house was used in this illustration. The titles "Mama and Papa" were used in this story because those are the names given to the authors by their grandson, Luke.

The Magical Reindeer were inspired by the author's first two adopted reindeer: Klaus (a boy) and Nutmeg (a girl). They were expecting their first baby (a girl named Snowflake) when they left the Snowman farm and "went to be with Santa at the North Pole". The book is dedicated to these beloved reindeer and the three stars on the final page are a tribute to their little family.